The LYON BEAR ™

KISS A ME PRODUCTIONS
COPYRIGHT 2002
ALL RIGHTS RESERVED
John Johnson - Illustration

Kiss A Me™ Productions, Inc. produces toys and booklets for children with an emphasis on love and learning.
For more information on how to purchase "The Lyon Bear"® collectible and plush toy
or to receive information on additional Kiss A Me products, write or call:

Kiss a me™ Productions

Kiss A Me Productions, Inc.
90 Garfield Ave.
Sayville, NY 11782
888 - KISSAME
888 - 547-7263

www.kissame.com

To *Theresa M. Santmann,*
A Leo in *Truth*

In a faraway forest quite near,
A big little bear shook with fear.
"Although I'm afraid,
I can be quite brave,
Especially when no one is here!"

All of the creatures would stare
At the big little bear they could scare.
When they would play,
He'd shout, "I will stay!"
Then swift run away like a hare.

His neighbors with neighborly whim
Kept trying to make him less grim.
But he wouldn't smile
Nor play for a while,
For in truth they terrified him.

He never tried to be brave,
He'd just hide out in his cave.
So the creatures there
Said, "He's a scaredy bear.
He doesn't know how to behave."

One bright day in the dark,
While sneaking alone through a park,
He said, "That's enough!
A bear's life is tough
But a lion's life must be a lark!"

"As a lion bear, when I wander near,
All creatures will tremble with fear.
They won't walk up and say,
'Hello, want to play?'
Or, 'Isn't that little bear dear?'

"I'll become a lion most foul,
With menacing tooth, claw and growl.
The animals at play
Will not want to stay
When I slink by on the prowl."

He decided a roar was the key.
A roar would make everyone flee.
"I'll have such a roar
They'll run for the door."
But the roar that he roared sounded WHEE!

That day he sat down to knit
A great lion's mane that would fit.
"I will practice each day
To scare others away.
I'll pretend if they stay, they'll get bit."

So he tied on his make-believe mane,
(Plus a buttoned-on tail he can't train).
But without a true roar
Who will run for the door?
For a lion with no roar is too tame!

With mane and tail he kept tryin'.
To be not a bear but a lion.
Yet a lion with a real mane
Would not whine and complain,
"WITH THIS MANE ON MY HEAD I AM FRYIN'!"

No one moved an inch nor a mile.
In fact they tried hard not to smile.
For that fake lion's roar
Sounded more like a snore
(The sound of a bear in denial).

His tail was a bit of a chore.
It too didn't work – like his roar.
It would get in his way,
Tripping him as he'd play
Or get caught on a tooth or a claw!

He prowled around night and day,
Trying to scare others away.
To please him they'd show
Pretend fear as they'd go,
But in truth they wanted to stay.

The animals grew tired of this game,
And cried out, "BEAR is your name!
It is time you must learn
To be honest and firm.
To insist you're a lion is lame!"

The bear in shame stood cryin'.
"You shouldn't all blame me for tryin'."
But the creatures were fair
And cried, "Never despair!
Just don't be a bear that is lyin'!"

Now...

Life should be more than a game.
We're meant to have courage not fame.
We each have the choice
To let truth be our voice.
To live life with truth is our aim!

THE END